My Old Grandad

Oxford University Press, Walton Street, Oxford OX2 6DP
Oxford London Glasgow
New York Toronto Melbourne Auckland
Kuala Lumpur Singapore Hong Kong Tokyo
Delhi Bombay Calcutta Madras Karachi
Nairobi Dar es Salaam Cape Town
and associated companies in
Beirut Berlin Ibadan Mexico City Nicosia

Oxford is a trade mark of Oxford University Press

First published in Austria by Verlag Jungbrunnen
© 1981 by Verlag Jungbrunnen, Vienna, Munich
© English version: Oxford University Press 1984

British Library Cataloguing in Publication Data
Harranth, Wolf
  My old grandad
  I. Title   II. Mein Opa ist alt. English
  833′.914[J]   PZ7
ISBN 0–19–279787–5

Phototypeset by Oxford Publishing Services
Printed in Austria

My Old Grandad

Wolf Harranth

Illustrated by Christina Oppermann-Dimow
and translated by Peter Carter

Oxford University Press
Oxford Toronto Melbourne

Our Grannie died. Poor Grandad was left all alone in the country.
So we asked him to come and stay with us in our town.
We met him at the railway station.
He came with a bashed-up suitcase
and a very old umbrella.

At home he sits in Daddy's place,
but Daddy doesn't complain.
Grandad does everything we are not allowed to do.
He smacks his lips when he is eating
and talks with his mouth full.

In the bathroom I've seen Grandad blow his nose
without a handkerchief!
He just blew his nose through his fingers.
I tried to do it but I couldn't.

And Grandad can take his teeth out of his mouth!
He puts them in a glass at night.
He is very old but I like him,
he smells so nice.

Grandad gets up very early in the morning,
just as the sun rises.
He walks up and down the room. Up and down, up and down.
When the floor-boards creak it wakes us up, too.
Grandad doesn't speak much.
Most of the time he just stands by the window
and stares down at the street.

Sometimes my little sister Katie is frightened of Grandad.
But she is only little.
I am big and strong.
I am never frightened. Well . . . sometimes I am. A *little* bit.

Why is Grandad so quiet?
Mummy says he is sad because Grannie is dead.
He stays in the house with us the whole day long,
full of sadness.
I think that Grandad doesn't like living in a town.

And he doesn't know that you should put your hand
over your mouth when you yawn.
But he does know how to mend a dripping tap —
and Mummy was going to pay a plumber!

Watching T.V. makes Grandad's eyes sore.
In the country he doesn't have television.
And he doesn't read books or
bother with the newspapers.

But Grandad likes my fairytales, and in the evening
he puts on his spectacles and reads them with me.
He reads slowly, saying the words,
and moving his finger along the line just like I do.

Yesterday Grandad did go out. He went to the Park.
He fed the pigeons but he said the roses needed pruning.
'Don't worry, the gardeners will do that,' Mummy said.
But early this morning Grandad crept out of the house.
When he came back, I was in the toilet and I saw him!
'Have you been pruning the roses?' I whispered.

Grandad laughed and put his fingers to his lips.
That was the first time he'd laughed in our house.
But don't worry, Grandad. I'll never tell on you. Never!

Sometimes I go shopping with Grandad.
He won't use the lift. No, he walks all the way up the stairs,
very slowly, one by one.

When we have to cross the street, Grandad holds my hand.
I hold him tightly, so he won't be afraid of the traffic.

In the supermarket he doesn't know what to do.
I have to help him. He says that in his village
he goes shopping with Mrs Smith.

But when the wheel came off my fire-engine,
Grandad took a tiny screwdriver in his great big hands
and screwed the wheel back on easily.
And Daddy can't do that.

Now Grandad has almost stopped eating anything,
and he doesn't speak at all, now.
He doesn't go out, not even to the Park.
Daddy looks at Mummy, Mummy looks at Daddy.
Why aren't they talking. . . ?

Suddenly Grandad's suitcase is packed,
and his old umbrella is on the top.
At breakfast Daddy says, 'Please stay longer.'
But Grandad just shakes his head slowly.
He is leaving.

Grandad gives me a toy farm, made of plastic.
Katie gets a big doll — but she doesn't like it!
In the kitchen Mummy says to Grandad,
'No, I don't want any money from you.'

At the railway station no one knows what to say
But as the train goes, I start sobbing.
'Come back, Grandad. I love you.'

Katie has cut off all her doll's hair!
Now she likes it, but Daddy is very cross.

Now Daddy sits in his own place again.
Mummy finds that Grandad has left some money
for her in the kitchen drawer.

I play with my farm.
In the countryside there are real horses to ride on.
'Mummy,' I ask, 'when will we go and see dear old Grandad?'